Peace in Our Time

Huang Yanhong

For Tyler, Jon, Kate, and Heidi

Thank you for teaching me.

Table of Contents

Christmas Night..9

December 26..13

December 27..21

December 28..29

December 29..39

December 30..51

New Year's Eve..61

New Year's Day...73

Author's Note..77

Christmas Night 2019

My audience murmured to themselves, seeing a thin teenager walk onto the stage. Cameras angled themselves in every direction, their lights almost too blinding for me to see. I adjusted my glasses and gripped the paper, holding on for dear life. The night was cold, but not bitter.

"Standing before you is the future." Dead silence. "Many generations went by under foreign rule. Soldiers landed on our shores, poured opium down our throats, and demanded payment. It was not until the One Country, Two Systems principle that we could live in peace, no longer under colonial powers. I ask you now - Where is your will? At this very moment, a regime attempts to steal the freedoms guaranteed to our forefathers. Are we not called once again to stand up in the face of an empire? To fight the injustice forced upon us? Before us is the future. A future in which all voices are heard, but one that those under the red and gold flag wish to quell. The time has come for our democracy to be tested. A free world will look to us in our time of trial, expecting us to rise from the ashes anew. Let us show them the power of the people. Free Hong Kong! Democracy now!"

I desperately gasped for air. The crowd applauded wildly, chanting my words back in unison, though I heard nothing. I knew it was time to go home. Every wall had graffiti on it, most shops either broken into or long evacuated. Occasional clashes between radical protesters and riot officers could be heard across neighborhoods. Lying in wait, police lurked outside my dorm.

My journey up the stairs was filled with scrolling through various forums. My jailbroken, highly illegal phone revealed all. In another part of the world, government loyalists were scrambling to get all evidence of me off Chinese servers. Mass takedowns and censorship blinded huge chunks of internet traffic that night, in part due to the rallying calls made by my associates and me.

"That kid knows what he's talking about!" said one public chatroom member.

"His brain's not fully developed yet," rebutted another.

"What will happen if we say we support him, do you

think?" a third said. "The people need to rise!"

"There was an American once said 'Injustice anywhere is a threat to justice everywhere.'"

"That was an American pig, who cares what they say."

"You all need help." That was the last message sent before the thread was closed by a moderator. Threads across the internet were flooded with similar debates, many of which were swiftly either locked or deleted.

Quietly stepping into my apartment, I pulled out my phone and nervously fumbled into "Contacts" to call my father, knowing it would go to voicemail. As I carefully cherished his voice on the playback greeting, an innocent knocking at the door was followed by the door splintering from the outside. Immediately surrendering with hands on my head and knees on the ground, the police blindfolded and cuffed their new prisoner.

Every officer spoke Mandarin, twisted in the ears of a young Cantonese-speaking activist. As the black veil was lifted, I found myself in an airtight interrogation room with a chrome one-way mirror on the left and a heavy steel door to the right

Two blue-uniformed officers with batons entered.

"Are you Kai?" the first officer asked.

"I answer to no puppet," I snapped.

"Just as we show no mercy to terrorists," the second officer provoked. I realized I was fastened to a chair, unable to move a limb. The first officer cracked his baton across my face, shattering my glasses. What remained of it rained onto the floor. The second hit came not a moment later, this time in my kneecaps.

Still reeling from the pain, I caught sight of the officers' uniforms. "Cadets? They sent cadets to detain me?"

Another baton hit struck my chest, leaving me breathless. "The People's Republic of China sent officers to quell a potential terrorist plot before it can unfold."

"What?" I exclaimed. "I'm simply a peaceful protester exercising my right to free speech."

"What?" I exclaimed. "I'm simply a peaceful protester exercising my right to free speech."

"Part of a larger plot to overthrow the president," the other officer accused while crouching to meet my eyeline.

"Part of a movement to keep Hong Kong out of his dictatorship."

"Rogue states get no voice," the officer stood up. "And just as unruly children are to be disciplined--" I cut off the cadet's monologue with spit grazing the officer's boot. Next thing I know, I came crashing to the floor, smacked across the face by a furious baton.

Barely conscious, I managed to scrape out one half of a sentence from my bloodied mouth: "...That among these are life, liberty, and the pursuit of happiness."

December 26

Kai was jolted awake by a splash of frostbitten water that almost felt refreshing on his wounds. It was early morning, about 4am., and he was now alone in a jail cell. I dismissed the officer and approached the table Kai was handcuffed to. His arms were chained behind his back, while his legs were tied with rope to his chair. As he started to awake, I composed myself to assert my dominance with a puffed chest and stoic posture. He looked younger than I imagined him.

"Kai Wu, I presume."

"It's Ng," Kai corrected as if he used that phrase all his life. "It's Cantonese, not Mandarin."

Taken aback by his calmness, I couldn't help but frown at him for a moment. "My name is Officer Fu Zhong. Do you know why you are here?"

"Because free speech is the enemy of the state?"

"Because there are many people above myself that believe that your friends are extremists. Make this easy on yourself."

"And do what? Sell out my friends who have done nothing wrong? We're not terrorists."

I chuckled to myself, legitimately unimpressed by his statement. "I'm sorry, you just reminded me of a joke. Want to hear it?" Unable to act for himself, Kai stared me down. I began to pace around the small room. It was storytime. "When I was in university, I had a professor who idolized the Communist Party. All of us did back then, but this one man was particularly loyal. One summer, news came of an uprising silenced by police, leaving a handful of extremists wounded. They called the government corrupt, tyrannical even. Word got twisted here and there, and all of a sudden, it was a massacre. People attacked police, police defended themselves, and people called it an injustice. Can you believe that? Return to my professor, who taught a Government class at the time, now proclaimed, 'One man's terrorist is another man's freedom fighter.' Security escorted him off the premises, and nobody heard from him for a week. You know what happened to him?" Silence. Kai was tearing up, yet frightened of interrupting the tale with the sound of his own sobbing. "He confessed to plots of assassinating all the major political heads in the People's Party. We found his body hanging under the bridge behind our school as a warning to all his students."

Kai was shaking wildly, unable to tell if it was out of crippling fear or the freezing water still dripping off him. "What now?" he cried.

I leaned over to Kai's ear, almost cheek-to-cheek and whispered "I will personally show you the full extent of what happens to you 'freedom fighters.'" With one swift movement, the officer reached over his side and swiped Kai's temple with his baton. Kai's head folded over, back in peaceful slumber.

Even I was impressed at how easy that was. I motioned for three guards to escort the unconscious body back to the nearby interrogation room. A fourth officer came behind the group, informing me of an incoming phone call. To our surprise, the call was coming from the United States Consulate in Hong Kong.

"Good morning, Mr. Ambassador," I greeted in my horribly accented English.

"Is this Fu Zhong of the People's Armed Police?" a female secretary replied.

"Speaking. My apologies, I was under the impression that I would be speaking to the ambassador himself. Please, associates use my English name, Frank."

"You will be connected to the Consul General in just a moment, however per his request, he would like to make sure that you are currently located in a private location with a secure connection."

"Of course," I lied. I was in a soundproof room with transcribers and higher-ranking officers listening in. No doubt that the ambassador would know this, it was a way of life. The Party must know everything about their servants.

"Very good. Please stay on the line." A gentle tune began to play, an unnerving placement, given the facility I was in. Soon, a new voice could be heard.

"Fu Zhong?" a foreign man asked.

"Frank. Consul, to what may I owe this pleasure?"

"You have nothing to worry about, officer. As your US diplomat, I assure you that I speak Mandarin quite fluently."

"Of course, I meant no disrespect."

"Let us move to more pressing matters rather than my language abilities." I rolled my eyes. "It has come under my attention that you have detained a rather interesting individual, a teenager?"

"Yes, sir, Kai Ng under suspicion of his involvement in terrorist scheming to overthrow President Xi and many leaders of the Communist Party."

"I'm aware, I have his file before me. However, what I do not see is any hard incriminating evidence. Kai's detention was caught on a video feed outside his apartment and spread through the news like wildfire."

I swore under my breath. How could those cadets let that happen? Who leaked it? Why does the ambassador have my prisoner's file? Why would he care about this particular case? "I don't understand, sir. What could be so important about the arrest of a teenager?"

"Well, for one, it occurred on Christmas night. People are outraged at the idea of arresting a former university student on holiday. Furthermore, he happens to be a former student of the Hong Kong Polytechnic University before its shutdown."

Taken aback by this revelation, I called for Kai's file. There it was in plain sight, a slight misstep on any number of people's fault. Footage from the siege on the university a month back made the protesters wildly popular, even if temporary. "That was something I was not made aware of. How bad is the backlash?"

"Awful. There's a crowd beginning to form outside the embassy calling for Mr. Wu's release."

"Wu? I'm sorry, is this the same student?"

"Undoubtedly. His name got mistranslated in the press, but that is beside the point."

"And that point is?"

"To formally ask you to release him. I must also ask that you disclose the detainee's location to the United States so that we may write an official press release."

Looking towards my discontented superiors, I formally denied the ambassador's request for release. I went on to disclose the name of the facility as a show of good faith between the homeland and the US. Upon hanging up, the commanding officers ordered me into the debriefing room. Inside were four members of the Communist Party, two of whom were particularly vocal.

"By the afternoon, we will have swarms of protesters at our gates," the warden cried angrily. "I would not even be surprised at some breaking into the facility to take matters into their own hands."

"Gentlemen, a break-in is the least of our problems," assured a Foreign Ministry representative. "This is a secure and heavily armed reeducation camp, any breach to our gates would be suicide."

"In any case," I dared to interrupt. "With this being such a high profile case, it has become my utmost priority to gain the information we need."

"I suggest that we extract the information as soon as possible," spoke the warden. "How much time do you need, Officer Zhong?"

"Give me a week. I will break him."

"Fine, January 2nd. If you are unsuccessful in your attempts, I will ask Agent Hong to intervene." The ministry envoy motioned towards a black-suited, elderly man speechlessly standing in the corner of the room. He was flipping around Kai's folder, taking careful notes of even the most minute details. Agent Hong was an operative of the Ministry of State Security, a a classified intelligence force within the Party.

"Your worries are in vain," I promised. "I will put in my best efforts and go beyond such."

The warden then dismissed the men, however, keeping me behind. "You understand the importance of this case, don't you, Frank? The very security of the President is at stake."

I sighed shakily and straightened my posture. "I expect a place for me in the Party after this is done."

"Of course, but remember..." The warden pulled me close and almost inaudibly finished his sentence - "Failure within the Party will not be tolerated. Much less with a matter so important to the President." I left for Kai's room.

I gazed into the interrogation room through a one-way window. Kai was still unconscious, strapped to the metal chair he was placed in during his arrival. Looking down, I found a manila folder with all recorded information the country had on Kai. Six days left.

Kai began to recuperate himself, evidently with some internal damage in his ears. Unlike the last time he was in this room, a new table was covered with riot suppression weaponry. I opened the door, file in hand.

"Zhong, was it?" Kai spat out.

"Before we begin, I must apologize," I started overlooking the arsenal. "When we last spoke, I only glanced over your file details, but it would seem that you are a much more interesting person than I first realized."

"Should I take that as a compliment?"

"Take it as you will," I replied. "Just know that you are my number one priority. So, talk to me."

"I know what you want, information that simply does not exist," Kai attempted to refute.

Skeptical, I returned to the profile. "It says here: 'Former student of Polytechnic University,' must have been quite an unfortunate experience."

"As if you care. We were sieged for almost two weeks inside our own school by the very police sworn to serve and protect. Have you ever watched as your community was showered with tear gas, rubber bullets, K9 units? Because I have."

I returned a sharp glare. "Listen here, your distraction tactics will not fool me. If you continue to refuse us information, I will break you, and nobody will get anywhere."

Kai sat up, still strapped in his metal chair, proud and

confident. "That is a sacrifice I am willing to make. Truth over injustice. When this is all done, I will have walked away with my pride, and you empty-handed."

Still determined to extract the necessary information, I called in two security guards and instructed that he be put in an eagle position, one of the most uncomfortable a human can be put in for hours on end, not to mention that which killed Christ. I turned to Kai once again, almost with the slightest amount of pity that was immediately extinguished. In English, I parted with a "Don't have too much fun without me."

Viewing from afar, I continued my experience from the one-way mirror's safety in the next-door gallery. I was surprised to find Agent Hong carefully jotting down deceptions and phrases used by both Kai and myself, most likely to gain an advantage in the scenario the Agent would be forced to intervene. The balding agent joyfully greeted me with an almost too friendly "Outstanding job, good sir."

"I gained nothing, there is much work to do, agent. Besides, do you not see observing this lowly activist as beneath you?"

Agent Hong held back his hearty laugh, only scraping out a chuckle. "Do you not see interviewing this potential terrorist and crushing his plot as your duty to this nation?"

Silenced, I sat beside the agent, a hopeless tactic to intimidate him. Even as he was being hoisted into the air, Kai continued with cries of "Free Hong Kong," "Silence is injustice," and the like. One of Kai's calls for help was eventually turned towards his parents as he screeched, "Mother, father, forgive me! Save me!"

Agent Hong took note of this call. "How useful was that?" I questioned.

"Potentially nothing, potentially everything."

"I try and not assign humanity to the inmates."

"Who said I was?" the agent corrected. "That call for his parental figures means that he has most likely wronged them in the past. Now that happens to be a point to exploit."

The day was now passing, and my patience began to

wane. Noticing night had fallen, I assumed the end of my shift and left Agent Hong and the guards to their own devices. Despite retreating for home, I knew I accomplished next to nothing in today's work. It was humiliating; however, tomorrow would come. I was greeted at the compound gates by dozens of protesters in Kai's name to my dismay. Barely slipping past the blockade, I was ever more determined to crawl into my welcoming bed. Strangely, calls began rolling in from journalists across the nation, asking for a comment, all of whom would have to wait until I actually cared.

December 27

I was nearly always first to punch into the front desk, and today was no exception. The halls were virtually silent, except for a single television playing the news in the front office. Initially, the newscaster was a white noise until mentioning a "Kai Wu." Sprinting to the front desk, I found the receptionist half alive from working the night shift.

"Turn that up," I commanded.

"Turn what up, Frank?" questioned the sleepy desk worker.

"Are you serious? What do you think? The only sound in the entire facility beside the prisoners."

"Would you call them prisoners or detainees?"

Confused as to why their conversation was taking so long to resolve, I reached over the desk and stole the television remote myself. Upon turning the volume up, I shocked myself to see the newscasters playing portions of Kai's Christmas speech.

"Confidence sounds pretty different than his screams for help, huh?" remarked the receptionist.

I proceeded to hurl the controller into the wall, shattering it. "Sorry about that, Jian," I apologized as I realized my actions. "I don't know what overcame me."

"Don't be," laughed Jian. "That was probably the most eventful thing that will happen at this desk all month. Anyway, the television is paid by the facility, so it looks like this happens to be neither of our problems now."

As I turned to stare at my feet, I found myself limping towards the interrogation room. Unsure of my own reasoning behind such slouching or the earlier outburst, I straightened my back and continued about the day. Before revealing Kai's most likely broken body, I found myself on an emergency call from Beijing. On the other line, a member of the Foreign Ministry was chewing my ear off for not extracting the information in the 24 hours between when they last spoke and now.

"I just fail to understand how I could have failed at this task if the deadline is still nearly the same as when you assigned it."

"When I give you an assignment, I expect its full completion even before whatever meaningless date I give you," spat the representative.

"With all due respect, representative," I began. "That is completely unreasonable. How can you expect such a difficult task to be finished with 100% thoroughness in such a short amount of time?"

"That sounded suspiciously like an act of defiance, Officer Zhong," remarked the offended envoy. "However, for your sake, I will be more 'reasonable' as you suggest. Your deadline is no longer January 2, as we first discussed. It is now December 30. Good day."

The phone's disconnect tone raised an uneasy feeling in my stomach. Attempting to hold my head up high, I began staring at the compound's surroundings through a frost-lined, bulletproof window. Across the open compound lot, to the entry gates, a massive crowd of about a hundred protesters that festered from a few dozens that amassed just yesterday. With the day still young, I watched the mob as it slowly awakened from their collective slumber, beginning to pick up their signs and harass anyone who attempted to enter or leave. I happened to be fortunate enough to check into work before enough activists awoke, but I knew my coworkers would not be so lucky. Before noon, news stations and government protective services alike will be on the scene. Any luck and police would disperse them by twilight.

Breaking his trance, Frank made his way towards the interrogation room. The janitor greeted him there, still wiping pools of blood off the concrete floor.

"Officer Zhong, how are you?"

"Good morning, Wei, doing well. Long night?"

Wei purified his crimson mop back to a stained white. "One of the most vocal guests we have had in a while. By the time the kid passed out, even the cadets wanted to get rid of him."

"Sounds like it was quite the night for Kai. Do you know if they were able to get anything?"

"Not by the sound of it, with how preachy our guest was being."

I took in my surroundings, noting the now reddened batons and blindfold. Wei tapped me on the shoulder, "You should check in with the guards, see what they have to say. Or the inmate, I'm sure any of them will have quite the story to tell. Speak of the devil."

As Wei talked, a man not much older than Kai strut into the room, arrogant and joyful. "Officer, to what do I owe the pleasure?"

"Remember your place, sir," I recalled. "You're a low rung on a tall ladder, a mere child compared to me."

"To be given such a low task," scoffed the guard. "Tormenting a political prisoner. And to be under the charge of somebody who entrusts such faith in cadets to detain and prepare a target."

"We serve the same president," I barked. "Yet, you stand here in defiance, attempting to order an officer. Do not test me. When I join the Party, do not expect my sympathy to be extended to you or the slightest memory of this interaction. Tell me what I want to know."

The guard glared at me, almost eyeing the ropes used on Kai, fantasizing about brutally breaking me. "We were able to have the prisoner sign this confession, pleading guilty to all charges." The confession was crumpled and dirty with shades of red, brown, and black. Original conditions printed on the paper could barely be read. Kai's signature could be identified on the margin, although shaky, misplaced, and almost illegible.

Taking the paper in hand, I folded it and placed it into my suit jacket. "Your efforts are appreciated. However, confessions do very little nowadays. That mob outside will not dissipate because of one paper. We need information."

"Then get it yourself," remarked the guard as he returned to attend his duties.

Down the hall of the interrogation room was the portal to the attached detainment block. While most prisoners were held in the general commons, where they slept on the floor, specially selected members were moved to the isolation block.

This particular facility could only hold a dozen detainees maximum, six on either side of the passage. Kai was the fifth, leftmost cell. More metal doors sealed the convicts in with a single, brick-sized window that was closed 90% of the time. Despite being metal, everything sealed so tightly that it might have been a padded cell in an asylum. Left in isolation, with just a single bucket and bed, prisoners were either given a choice to leave with their lives or their pride.

Four guards helped escort me through the common area, as to not be disturbed on my mission. The familiar, yet low chatter of the common area was interrupted by the rusted door hinges in Kai's chamber. Kai himself was wrapped in his thin bedsheets, attempting to escape the frigid and stale air with sleep. Now awoken, but tremendously tired, Kai began to sob. "Officer Zhong. Frank. Please do not steal me from this oasis. I have never known true terror until last night, imagining what the rest of my days will be like."

Blood painted the interior of the dungeon in the form of spatters, handprints, and pools. I could barely manage to withhold my disgust brought on by both sight and smell. The only solace I had was to remind myself of Kai's status as an enemy of the State. "Get up," I commanded. Kai tussled in his sheets, whispering faint prayers to himself. I armed myself with a riot baton, expecting resistance. "Do not make this harder for either of us."

Kai inched out of his cell on all fours like a wounded dog, despairing events to come. I proceeded to trample Kai's already broken hand to assert dominance. In my utility belt, I carried a pepper-spray lined blindfold to carefully apply to prisoners' eyes. The painful burn rashed Kai up to his brows, instinctually causing crying. Anticipating the natural body spasm as a reaction to the agony, I angled my feet so that Kai could not move, with my free leg now on his lower back. Once he started to settle, I cuffed him. Removing my left foot from Kai's lower back and right foot from Kai's right hand, I proceeded to lift Kai to his feet via his crimsoned shirt collar.

Eyes peered out the other cells, some more injured than others, to investigate the racket. Kai's sharp voice and pained groans had drawn the attention of the entire common area as well. Still carrying Kai by his shirt, I attempted to force Kai's bruised legs to stand on their own by dragging them across the floor. Unresponsive, Kai's lead body simply slumped over like a corpse. On our way to the interrogation room, onlookers observed from across the room. After an eternity of clumsy transportation, I launched him into the same metal chair I knew Kai loved. Lethargic and now staggering from the repeated head trauma, Kai no longer resisted much.

With all his limbs tied to the sadistic throne, Kai turned his eyes to his captor. "That was cruel," he whispered.

I, who was almost breathless, fired back with a scowl. "Maybe if you had lifted your knees off the ground, maybe it would have been less so."

"Do you know how long they left me hanging in this room?"

"Not my problem. Your pain is a result of your actions. Tell us what we want to know, or you burn at the stake. We already have your confession."

Kai quietly shook his head. "What will your forced confession buy you? Because it certainly will not get you any surrenders."

"The next time you see the outside of these walls will be in a body bag, I do not doubt that," I spat. "However, before you are even granted such grace, you will give me what I seek."

"I'm just a kid," Kai began before slowly being sapped of his energy from his anger. "What will people think if I die under your supervision? Nothing will have been achieved, and I think that means something. No compromise, no reward. For either of us." Kai's head fell back as his exhaustion overcame him.

Most likely suffering internal bleeding, I called the faculty doctor for Kai. I could not discern whether this call was a sign of determination, fear, or genuine worry. I contemplated Kai's words to strike a balance. However, a call from the front desk broke this train of thought as there was apparently a woman on hold for me.

"Hello?"

"It's me," the witch replied. "When you get home from work, I'll be waiting inside."

"Wait, you disappear for three years, and that's what you start with? What is this even about?" No response. Some rustling on the other end was interrupted by a white tone that left more questions than answers. All I knew was that my estranged ex-wife, who was once thousands of kilometers away, was now just a twenty-minute drive into the city.

Jian, the desk flunky, interjected. "Past lover?"

Disgusted, I immediately cauterized the conversation before it could start. "Close, but no. Mind your own business."

"What happens at my desk is my business. You can trust me."

"Can I? Since when? The only time we interact is when I choose to greet you on my way in and out."

"Come now, you know nothing happens around here. Tell me about what's going on with you."

"Stop. I'm busy, let me get back to work."

I returned to the interrogation room, with a revived Kai sitting before me. As the doctor shut the door behind them, leaving just the duo alone, a mutual glare was exchanged.

"And now what? You call a medic to keep me from dying but have no use for me in life. Might as well have let me choke on my own blood."

"You know I cannot let you do that. I will save you, again and again, only to put you through Hell, again and again, if it means getting anything and everything you know."

"What a waste of energy to do such a futile task. By the time I die, the riots will be over, and the Party will have fallen."

I refrained from further violence. Kai had taken blow after blow now, one more would be just a single grain on the hill already placed. "I guess it's back to the cell with you." I needed to do something though- the information I needed was in that head somewhere, just in need of a bit of shaking. "What shall I add next? Eagle position? Singing the anthem? How about I remove your bed and bucket?"

December 27 (Late Afternoon)

At the end of the hallway was Frank's apartment, directly across from the elevator entry with a glass walkway in between. For a good few hours, I waited for him, admiring the grand view that could be seen from Frank's private skywalk. Absolutely crushed from exhaustion, Frank limped out of the elevator to carry him to his sanctuary apartment. I knew Frank was a firm believer that hard work should be rewarded with blissful rest, separated from the twisted work he was ordered to do daily. As he arrived at his most likely government-issued suite, he tried to ignore me.

"Hello, Frank," I greeted in a neutral tone from down the hall.

"Zhen. Never thought I'd find you waiting for me at home ever again."

"Did you not receive my call? And it's Jenny now."

"I recognized your scaly voice anywhere," Frank passive-aggressively mentioned. "Jenny? So Americanized."

"Grow up. You think sucking up to the regime is the future? You're as old-world minded as you once were when I first met you."

"And you think the Americans are so progressive?" he antagonized. "They do the same things, just swept under the rug. Don't give me that mask of righteousness. I can only imagine how the children are doing."

"Don't you dare speak of my kids as if they're yours too," I slapped him across the jaw. "I gave them an escape from your hubris, Frank. They live a life in luxury, distant and a world apart from your miniature game of 'Soldier.'"

"I'm guessing your arrival reasons are lower than insulting me, so just get it over with, you--"

I pulled a newspaper from my coat, with headlining text spelling out "HERO BOY ARRESTED BY HK POLICE." Frank groaned as he dropped it to the floor, forcing me to sweep it back up. "Word spreads to the United States fast. And the news does love a good hero story, no matter whether it ends in victory or martyrdom."

"Piece of filth deserved it if you ask me."

"Well, no-one did. You may not believe it, but I'm here on diplomatic duty."

"On whose authority?" Frank angrily enquired.

"You could say on behalf of the millions of citizens now under the fist of Mao."

"Nice, I knew working for the Americans would buy you some dignity someday," he remarked sarcastically. Frank pushed me out of the way to make way to his way to the apartment.

I barely caught the door open as he almost slammed it shut. "Listen, I'm begging you, please release him. He's not even old enough to drink."

"Maybe not in the United States, but you're not there now. We play by a different set of rules. The boy knew the risks and took them anyway, so here he is, paying the price."

"Sure, but everybody knows you're in charge of him. Read the fine print," I pointed at the newspaper. Upon further inspection, Frank would find his own name in print from leaked documents and a US Embassy source. I hoped that seeing him being thrown under the bus would change his mind.

"What happens now?"

"'What happens now?' You either face the people or the Party. Make the right decision. For me, for the kids. Set an example."

I shut the door on Frank's foot, causing him to fall back and reel in pain. He no longer had my pity, especially if he was persecuting protesters. As I found myself on the ground floor, I looked outside to see that a few protesters were scouting the area. They most likely found Frank's address and are out for blood, but I knew he would be fine. The best security in China, right on Frank's doorstep. That's the power influence buys you.

December 28

"What's this? Where am I?" I called out into the abyss.

"Start singing," I heard over and over again. If I could just slip into the night, I could escape reality.

"What?"

"The National Anthem. Start singing."

I began to sing what I knew of the American National Anthem, which was particularly hard to do since I never studied hard in my English classes.

"Wrong! The National Anthem of the Motherland. Of the Party. It will help reawaken your senses."

It was as if they were trying to brainwash me, but I'd sooner get smothered a hundred times over than taint my tongue with those words. A guard broke open a door, which poured light into the dark cell for the first time in what seemed like years. He shoved me to the floor, and the night turned to a blurry haze.

Suddenly, the cold stone floor my face was against turned to carpet. The velvety cloud smelled like cigarettes and home-cooked stew. It was dinnertime, and it was my turn to set the table. But I had fallen asleep on the ground. Father will be mad.

Yet, there he is, sleeping with the TV on again. He looks so peaceful after work, now that he can just lay back. His eyes grew heavy, Mom's did too, and so were mine. I heard a dog barking, but we never had one.

I was awoken with the feeling of falling. The black bag was removed from my head, and my retinas were burned by the morning sunlight. It took me a moment to recover from the natural flashbang that went off in my face, but it wasn't long until I came back to my senses. I was being dangled over the building roof with a few K9 units foaming at the mouth a few stories down. I tried not to react, and the guards lost their patience, pulling me back to the rooftop's safety, splashed cold water on my crotch.

Finally, when I could fully appreciate my surroundings, Frank sat across from me once again alongside two guards.

This time, however, we were not in the jail cell. Instead, we were on the facility's rooftop, with two more guards holding the chair I sat in and the now-empty bucket of cold water, respectively. Obviously, I was still strapped to the same old metallic chair.

"You seemed to get quite comfortable after spending your night in the Isolation Chamber."

"Is that what it was? I thought I was on vacation."

"I see you continue to joke about your situation, which only tells me you need more time in the Chamber. Maybe this time in the eagle position or with a few uniformed friends to keep you company. Come back when you're willing to talk."

Two guards placed a black bag over my head and began to drag me from behind, so I couldn't see where I was going. "Wait!" I called from beneath the mask. "Maybe we can compromise." It was a last-ditch effort. I had no chips to bet, but that also meant I had nothing to lose.

"Mr. Ng, you are in no position to negotiate. I believe we had a similar conversation to this just yesterday."

"Maybe if you just treated me like a human being, you'd see where I'm coming from."

Frank paused to ponder something before returning to me. "What is it that you want?"

"Why do you care? It's doubtful you could even get me the things I want."

"Humor me."

The four guards looked at each other in disbelief and removed my bag blindfold. My chair was placed flat across from Frank. "First," I started, "I want your guarantee that no harm will come to me or my family."

"And in exchange for that, you will give us the names of your cohorts?"

"No, I'm just setting the ground level. I just want your word."

"If I make such promises, you must be confident in your information. How do I know you're worth my time?"

I thought for a moment before speaking up again. "I'm just a kid from PolyU fighting for what's right. I have no doubt that you would defend China against enemies at the gates, so how do you think we feel?"

"Unfortunately for you," Frank motioned for us to be moved. "Hong Kong was never a country. It's a city to be subjugated under power, which it will always be because there's no reason to change."

One of the guards began to drag my chair from behind to somewhere I could not see. "You say that, and yet, you refuse to look at the people, the city's culture, or even the local government. It's far too different from being integrated into your 'People's Republic.'"

The blindfold was placed over my eyes, most likely to prevent me from understanding my surroundings, thus preventing my escape. I found myself back in the interrogation room, chained to the table once more. The rattling sound the cold metal made rubbing against itself had now felt so familiar.

Frank pulled up a chair to sit across from me. For what felt like the first time, I felt like I was being seen by an actual person, and not by a puppet. "You remind me of my father," I broke the silence.

"How so?"

"When I did something bad, my father used to drag me to the living room to scold me. Sometimes he'd beat me if the offense was bad enough. I never learned, though."

"Learnt what?"

"How to bow to authority. To strength. No matter how much he'd scold me or beat me, I would never apologize."

"True remorse cannot be brought out by fear or pain."

That's what I wanted to hear. With any luck, maybe Frank would loosen my restrictions. With a little more grease, perhaps I could even free myself. "Empathy. Understanding. A willingness to listen. All things my father deprived me of."

"We're off-topic," Frank cut me off. He was clearly interested in the conversation, but something was stopping him. He was a puppet after all, and somebody behind him was still pull-

-ing strings. I felt sorry for him. Maybe I could free him as well.

"Are you a father?"

Frank hesitated, a nerve was struck. "Yes, two boys."

"I was an only child. We had a happy life until the protests."

"What happened to your parents?"

"They disowned me after I took the side of the people. Their nationalism got in the way of their sense of justice." Why was I telling him this? He's the enemy.

"Politics often does get in the way of one's personal life. Differing opinions can split lives." Frank sounded sullen. Could it be that he lost someone close to him in a similar matter to mine?

"Similar ones can create communities."

"And what kind did you join?"

I tensed up. My friends had done nothing wrong, and yet I knew if I sold them out, they would be arrested on false charges. "I know you think they did something bad. Or are planning to. You're wrong, we're peaceful."

"There's plenty of footage online and across the media of you protesters assaulting various citizens and officers, sometimes even murdering them. Not to mention defacing and destroying public property. We could easily charge you with all of these. I'm sure you would choose those over treason."

"But I would have to sell off my friends. My innocent friends."

"Who knows, maybe some of them aren't as innocent as they would have you believe. None of them are coming for you, and none of them will save you now. The only thing that should be on your mind right now is confession."

"I've never participated in that, nor have my friends as far as I have witnessed. There is nothing to confess to. Do you expect me to make something up?"

Frank nodded. "It's for the greater good. Plus, it's not like them being on the outside can help you. Their arrests will take time off yours. That I can guarantee."

Surely these were interrogation tactics. Why would this officer stick his neck out for me just to take time off my stay? "How can I trust you?"

There was a vague sense of sadness from Frank as he stared into my eyes. "Listening to you now, you remind me of my oldest son. He was headstrong like you."

"Was?"

"I haven't seen him in over four years. My ex-wife took him and his brother to America when we divorced."

I thought about how he was talking to me, like a friend. What kind of interrogation was this? Or what had it turned into? I don't know how long I sat in silence, pondering these questions. "What my friends and I are doing is right. I will not debate that. Does it justify murder? Never, but when there is no justice, there shall be no peace."

Frank sat back in his chair, disappointed. He probably felt that he was getting somewhere. "Have you heard of the expression, 'Debate not to win, but to understand?'"

"A nice expression, but a useless one."

"Rigidity and hubris will get us nowhere."

"Neither will your nationalism," I said under my breath.

"Please understand, we don't want to keep you here, but you will not talk this through."

"Me? I was the one who was thrown in a cell. Who was forced to sit in darkness in an eagle position and singing the national anthem? Who ordered such things?"

Frank looked uncomfortable. I had hoped that he regretted his treatment of me. Finally, he stared me dead in the eyes and asked me, "Why do you fight?"

December 28 (Late Afternoon)

Six years ago, I went on vacation to Los Angeles in the United States with my family. None of us had ever been this far from China; however, we liked that. It was liberating in its own strange way. I couldn't believe how diverse and yet separated the people could be, it was paradoxical. Somehow, it reminded me of home.

During our stay, my older son was adamant on finding a library, for reasons I didn't understand. I was opposed to it, but Jenny took him to one. Apparently, they filled themselves with knowledge of texts banned back home, readily available in America. Jenny especially found some comfort there, explicitly choosing the free computers to explore the unrestricted internet.

A few months later, on our anniversary, Jenny surprised me with a gift, an American laptop. She told me that installed on it was a virtual private network, something to bypass filters and restrictions at home. She also gave me a list of sites and keywords to use to educate myself. At the time, I refused it, knowing that such technology would be dangerous and contradictory to the anti-American values I had been taught. The contraband sat idle in my drawer since I was too unsure of myself to actually dispose of it. Today, however, it would come into use.

The laptop was out of date, still using the last operating system. After a brief recharging and update, I was ready. Using the list that was bundled with the computer and the private network, I began my own research to understand more about the outsider's perspective on the Party, China as a whole, the Hong Kong situation, among other topics.

My dive took me until long past dark, and by the time I pulled myself away, I felt overloaded with information. There was more to uncover, but I supposed there would be time for those revelations to come another day. A text notification appeared on my phone, and to my surprise, it came from Jenny.

"Saw you accessed the REAL internet," it read. "Aren't you going to dig deeper?"

"How did you know that?" I replied. "You did something to this laptop, I know it." I considered burning the laptop. If found, the information searched on it would be incriminating.

"You've always been a traitor."

"So hostile, Frank." I couldn't help but read that in her smug tone. "Just know that there is always more than what lies on the surface. Beware creatures that lurk beneath it, however."

"What was that supposed to mean?" No response. If she had laid a trap for me, I fell right into it.

December 28, 2013 (Six Years Ago)

My father, Fu, had always been a stubborn man. He wanted nothing to do with America, other than visiting for a leisurely vacation. When we suggested visiting local sites to educate ourselves, he saw no benefit.

"Look, I love Dad," I started. "But he won't listen to reason."

"Baby," Mom comforted, petting my head. " I love him too and someday, he will. He just needs a good shaking."

"Just the two of us? We may be his family, but we both know how he can be."

Mom sat beside me and gave a big hug, sitting on the hotel bed. "Your father has a thick skull, but even he can be brought to reason. When we move here, whether he likes it or not, it'll be for good."

I stood up, pacing the room. "I want Dad to come with us, I really do. He just can't see we're trying to help him."

"Sometimes," she started. "Stubborn people need a good jolt awake. Your father will get his soon, I'm sure of it."

Still skeptical, I asked, "But what can I do to speed it up? There must be something. I've tried talking to him before."

"What happened then?"

"He wouldn't budge, saying something about 'even though you're my son, I cannot compromise.' What kind of person, what kind of father, doesn't listen to reason to this extent?"

There was a knock at the door. I could hear my younger brother through the door, complaining about walking so much. Mom got up from the bed, walking towards the door. "We'll finish this later, baby. We'll try and convince your father during this trip. If that doesn't work, we'll keep trying. Just keep your head up."

"Honey, are you in there?" I heard my Dad call from behind the heavy hotel door.

"Somewhere inside him is the amazing father I once knew," I sighed. "Someday he'll come back to replace the prideful fake. I just hope it's not on his deathbed."

December 29

"Good morning, Frank," Jian greeted. "Is something wrong?"

My eyes had bags sagging under them. My arms drooped and almost dragged my briefcase on the floor. Due to last night's events, I had not gotten nearly enough sleep. "Long night, lots of paperwork."

"From the Party, I assume? Your case is of the utmost importance. Speaking of which, I need to check that."

"Of course." One of Jian's top priorities was hand-inspecting materials officers like myself brought in as the desk clerk. My briefcase was a usual sight as I always kept essential documents in it. However, today I was sneaking in a bit of contraband.

Jian scanned the innards of the case. "That's a nice notebook," he commented. "Here you go."

I can't imagine what would have happened if he dared peer into the notebook. Detainment? Interrogation? "Thanks, see you later."

"Actually, can I grab you for a second?"

Not wanting to raise suspicion, I put up a fake smile. "What is it?"

"Agent Hong wanted me to give this to you." Jian handed me an envelope, stamped with a special seal.

I placed the envelope into my case and thanked Jian again. There was a staff lounge nearby where I was able to find some solitary to inspect the letter. The seal was of the National Emblem; however, I had never seen it used in this fashion. I almost felt that I was violating the letter somehow by opening it. The message read as follows:

"Greetings Officer Fu Zhong.

I would like to preface this by thanking you for your continued service to the People's Republic. This letter serves as proof that upon completing your latest assignment, which is now classified as a 'civic duty,' you will be elevated from your current position. While I cannot guarantee your exact future placement, I can state that you will be more than satisfied with the utmost assurance. We have made a celebratory dinner reservation tonight after your shift at the compound ends. A designated vehicle will pick you up to escort you to the restaurant. We anticipate your cooperation.

Signed, Agent Hong Cuo of the Ministry of State Security"

My stomach sank. For the past few hours, I felt nothing except the notion that I may be living a lie: this government, its party, its citizens. I dared not think about what would happen if they found the laptop or the notebook. Now they want me to eat with them? No doubt they're asking for a status update on Kai, which I don't have much to report. My situation was worse, considering tomorrow's deadline. I shuddered at the thought of what would happen if my job were to miss its mark.

Regardless, I gathered my emotions and ordered some guards to bring Kai to the interrogation room. Per his request, Kai had been moved from the isolation chamber to the common area. I knew my superiors would disapprove, however, I thought it necessary. With the suspect now more cooperative, it will be easier to extract the information.

"You look tired, long night?" questioned Kai as he sat strapped down.

"Research. I wanted to better understand your circumstances."

"That sounds strangely treasonous, but I hope you get it now. Our cause is just."

"Depends on where you sit, always has." I glanced at his situation. "And it does seem that one of us is better off than the other."

"One of us is in chains for fighting for beliefs," he rebutted. "I live by a belief of justice."

"Justice? Is that what you call attempted murder of lawmakers? Or the protests of a law allowing criminals to be sent to the mainland to be tried by the law's fullest extent?"

Kai was fuming at the ears. "Hong Kong has a perfect trial system, there is no reason to try them in China. Besides, unlike our balanced system, yours is corrupted and in favor of the government rather than the people."

"The government protects people from themselves, and our means make sure that no danger breaches public safety."

"By restricting free speech? Allowing for open arrests? What a joke."

"Think of it as disciplining a child. A child cannot should never act on his own will without the guidance of his parents. He could hurt himself, or worse. Precautions are necessary to protect the greater good, even if that means imprisoning such vocal critics like yourself."

"The very nature of children is to grow and begin to think like an adult," Kai responded. "You cannot take our rights and expect us to stand idle. First, our judicial systems and free speech, then what? Soon we'll be left as another puppet state unless we act now."

I was taken aback by his tenacity and decided to recall my notes from last night. Summoning my briefcase, I removed Kai's file, my journal, and a pen, placing all three on the table. "These are extremely sensitive documents. You should count yourself lucky.

Kai rolled his eyes. He read his name on the folder and curiously peered at the journal. "That's a new journal, although judging by the weary pages, you probably have been using it quite a lot."

"Perceptive," I remarked. "These are my personal notes on current issues. Officers like myself must keep up with the changing times."

"You didn't seriously bring debate notes to this interrogation, did you?"

A bit flustered, I began to flip through the notebook. I turned to a page with prominent protester names and showed it to Kai. "Which ones are you involved with?"

Kai glanced at the list. "None of them, my friends and I act alone," he disregarded.

"Really? You and your friends alone were able to broadcast you across the world? You must have some powerful frien-

-ds."

"You speak of the changing times, however, ignore to see the obvious." Kai leaned into his chair. "Activism is easier now more than ever. Cameras, the internet, streaming, it's all connected. It doesn't take more than a simple rally posting and a phone to record the action."

"What about the news stations?"

"Nearly all of them were international teams, usually just a host and a cameraman. We just sent a tip to the stations ahead of time that we were going to make a spectacle."

"And that was?"

"The rallying cry of a young teenager, silenced by an iron fist," Kai smirked. "And it worked perfectly."

"Everything was planned?" I thought for a moment, staring at Kai's folder. "That's how your arrest was caught on camera despite our ambush."

"I'd hardly call that clumsy raid 'an ambush,'" Kai cockily laughed. "Planning and a little luck was all we needed."

I needed to change the subject, pulling a document from the folder. "Your parents." Silence. "They're not in Hong Kong, are they?"

Kai's smile turned into a glare. "Leave them out of this."

"You may be a legal adult, but they're still your next of kin, no matter how estranged you may be."

"I hate them," Kai confessed. "They never understood what I fought for. They just wanted me to sit still while our freedom was stripped away. But, how can one sit passively by as their very flesh is torn from their bones?"

Somehow this remark gave me mixed feelings. While I admired the tenacity, I started to get annoyed by this sense of righteousness Kai seemed to always have. "I find it interesting how you say you hate your parents; however, you called for them a few days ago, remember? What did you do to make you ask for their forgiveness?"

Kai hesitated. "It was worse between my father and me. However, I said some things to my parents I didn't mean, and they said some things back. There's nothing else to it."

"And this relates to the protests?"

"Somewhat. I wanted to study at Polytechnic because I always thought it was an exceptional school; however, my father wanted to send me to Beijing. He wanted me to become a lawyer, politician, or something of the sort, and I disagreed. I threatened to move to America, there was a lot of yelling, but I ended up storming out. I haven't seen them since."

"And you ended up at PolyU?"

"My friends went there, put in some good words with the admissions office, and I was given a last-minute entry. That's when the protests hit. Seems like I couldn't escape politics even if I tried."

Yunzi, my older son. I haven't seen him since Jenny took him to America five years ago. Kai's words remind me of him. I reminisced on the past a bit before being interrupted by a knock on the door. Agent Hong peered in to end the session, due to an apparent "emergency." Kai was quickly hauled back to his detainment area while Hong and I conversed.

"What's the emergency?"

"There is none," laughed the scruffy agent. "I thought you just needed a break, so why don't you and I get some lunch?"

"This is serious, Agent. I need to get the information out of him by tomorrow, you know that."

"I'm serious too. We have important matters to discuss that involve the dinner tonight."

After a bit of convincing, I eventually found myself at a local cafe with Agent Hong. He covered the price of both our meals just to be polite before we started talking again. "Now, will you fill me in on whatever this is?"

Agent Hong put his cigarette out and his coffee down. "Tonight, you will be meeting with two of my superiors. First impressions are everything, and they matter the most when meeting veteran Party members. That being said, what is your progress on the child?"

"Everything's coming together, I assure you. However, I admit things are moving slower than I anticipated."

"The Party expects your success by tomorrow night, Frank. Otherwise, I'll be forced to intervene. Is there anything I can do at the moment to assist you?"

"Anything you got from him due to me is enough, I think. You have been watching, haven't you?"

Hong relit his cigarette. "Of course, it's my duty as the next level above you. Don't worry, if I succeed due to your information, I'll be sure to share the glory."

Something about that still left me uneasy, how I could just not try, and Hong would finish the work for me. "Thank you, Agent Hong."

"Please," he started. "It's my pleasure. Let's just enjoy our meal."

December 29 (Late Afternoon)

The rest of my day was spent doing paperwork, solving cadet problems, and vetting new detainees. More journalists began calling again after telling them I wasn't making comments, so I ignored them. Kai was still resistant, so, unfortunately, we had to move him back into the isolation chamber indefinitely. While I understood his position better now, I could not tolerate his actions. At around 7pm, a black van stopped in front of the compound. Out emerged Agent Hong, who came to fetch me to take us to the venue.

While the outside of the van looked standard, the interior of the car was fully customized. Like a compact limousine, the inside was basically a small club lounge squeezed into a vehicle. The one-way windows made it wholly private and had plenty of legroom for guests to stretch. For younger guests, the van's roof could also be moved, allowing for a luxurious experience.

Except, I couldn't relax now. Awaiting me in the van was one of the two men I was meeting that night, a Foreign Ministry representative that I had only briefly conversed with a few days ago.

"Officer Zhong, is it? My name is Minister Nam. A pleasure to meet you, comrade."

He was a stout man with a pitch-black overcoat covering his navy suit. He didn't look entirely Chinese, which threw me off. A single pin was on his lapel, that although slightly obscured, I recognized as the hammer and sickle. "The pleasure is mine." I shook his hand as the car began to move.

"I hope you don't mind, Officer, but the Agent and I were just discussing a private matter. Would it be fine with you if we finished it?"

"By all means," I politely gestured. To my surprise, Nam and Hong then continued conversing in Korean. Even then, it didn't sound like the regular dialect, like ones I've heard at Korean restaurants or shows. From the limited amount I knew from my school days, I understood two phrases: "understand" and "inform."

When they finished about ten minutes later, Nam was

the first to include me with the occasional glances. "Hong has informed me that you're looking for a spot in the Party. May I ask why?"

There wasn't any particular reason why I just wanted the status. "I suppose," I started. "I'm looking for a more comfortable lifestyle, one that deals with more elegant people."

"Elegant? I suppose etiquette isn't too common among youngsters these days?" Nam chuckled. "Why did you become an officer then? Would it not have been more direct to go into business?"

"My father was an officer. He taught me to protect and serve my country from a young age."

"Then why not join the military?" Hong chimed in.

"Honestly, I never liked the idea of handling weapons. It may seem roundabout, but I enjoyed the idea of enforcement and elevating myself to Commissioner. However, as the years went by, I realized that I wanted to secure myself with more political power like you, Minister."

"Comfortability and power, huh?" Nam rubbed his thinly bearded chin. "That can be arranged."

The van began to pull up to the restaurant, which turned out to be an expensive fusion steakhouse on the outskirts of Hong Kong. It was distant from the protests, however, so the building and the surrounding district was intact. Sitting at one of the far booths browsing his menu was a frail, elderly man with round glasses and a thick beard. He looked foreign as well, except he seemed more Caucasian.

"Excuse us, Ambassador," Nam interrupted. "May I introduce to you our guest tonight, Officer Fu Zhong."

December 29 (Night)

The ambassador stood up, using his cane as support, to shake my hand. "Greetings, dear sir. Ambassador Volkov, at your service." His raspy voice was like a harsh smoker dry heaving his breaths. His Mandarin, while fluent, sounded like it had a northern accent.

"It's an honor, Ambassador," I replied. Agent Hong sat beside Volkov, while Nam took the one across from them. Leaving a spot for me, I was terrified to be squished between two powerful politicians who could decide my entire future.

"By all means," Volkov spoke up as I began scanning the menu. "Eat however you wish tonight, the owner of this fine establishment is an excellent friend of mine."

Agent Hong signaled the waitress over with an annoyed demeanor. The woman hastily rushed over as fast her skirt and heels would allow her. Her face, while smiling, obviously had eyes of discontentment. "Ready to order, sir?"

"I'll have the rare Kobe fillet with the side of scallops and dumplings." The waitress began making her way around the table for orders.

Nam thought for a moment, staring intently at his menu. "I suppose I'll have the Korean-style abalone bowl with fried shrimp."

She came to me next, and I was a bit flustered. "Just the roast goose and egg tart for me."

Volkov smiled warmly at the waitress. "Just the pork and beef rice bowl, thank you. May I add shark-fin soup and wine for the table too?" The waitress, while still uneasy, escaped away to the kitchen to place our order. While I thought our respective choices in meals were interesting, I didn't think much of it. Volkov began to turn his attention to me. "Zhong, is it? May I call you Frank?"

Although forward, I couldn't deny his request as his subordinate. "I'd be honored."

"Frank, I must say, your file was quite promising. I believe all of us are familiar with its potential. Are you confident in your skills?"

"I always put my best foot forward, sir, and I'm grateful for your praise."

"But, are you confident?" Minister Nam chimed in. "Unconfident people with extraordinary abilities never go far."

"I suppose so," I mustered up. "My skills have got me this far, they haven't seemed to fail me yet."

"Let's say this latest case of yours fails," proposed the ambassador. "Would you still be confident then?"

"I believe my decisiveness will prove victorious in the end."

Nam took an interest in this. "Decisiveness? Does that mean you're on the edge of a breakthrough?"

"It hinges on a few choices, but I'm sure victory is at hand." My assurance put the room at ease. Despite this, I heavily doubted my results.

Hong was clearly skeptical; however, his attention quickly shifted. "You there! Who are you?"

Afraid, the man watching from behind the counter emerged slowly and approached the table. He was an older man, like me, except he wore a white and purple dinner jacket. Volkov immediately recognized him. "Don't bother him, Agent. This is Mister Rong, he's the owner of this fine establishment.

"Ambassador, lovely to see you." Rong faked a smile, glaring at Volkov. "As always, your meal is completely covered by the house, so you gentlemen enjoy your night." Rong quickly managed to excuse himself, most likely to avoid an uncomfortable discussion.

"My apologies, Officer," Agent Hong started as the food was beginning to be served. "This dinner is supposed to be about you, our esteemed guest."

"I almost forgot," laughed Volkov. "Let's celebrate your upcoming success."

Nam motioned over to Volkov, to which the minister whispered something in the ambassador's ear. I only managed to make out the word "suspicion." The two men looked at me from across our small booth and returned to their natural posture.

"Is something wrong, dear sirs?" I asked.

"No, no," the ambassador dismissed. "Nam was just telling me of your planned future with the party. We can toast to that." The waitress from earlier returned with four glasses and a bottle of aged wine. I only caught a glimpse of its price, which was more than three months of my salary.

Upon pouring, another waiter came from the sidelines with our food. Hong was practically drooling on the floor. "Ambassador, will you please make the toast? I believe we'd all like to taste this delectable meal."

Volkov patted his uniform down and raised his glass, to which we matched him. "To Officer Zhong. May his father, grandfather, and forefathers look down upon him in pride for his service to the Party will be true and everlasting. Loyal and undying. Unwavering and dauntless. To Fu!"

The three men drank heartily, Nam and Hong nearly emptying their entire glass in a single swig. Meanwhile, I decided to take a sip, knowing that it would be in my interest to remain sober, especially among my superiors.

After finishing our meal, a call came from an unknown number; however, I recognized it from earlier in the afternoon. This time, I'd tell them to leave me alone.

"Is this Frank?" a woman inquired.

"Speaking. Do you know this is my private number? Only personal matters are supposed to reach me, so if this about the news-"

"This is Dr. Yang of the Caritas Medical Centre in Hong Kong. Your wife, Jenny, was brought into our emergency care ward this past evening. Will you please stop by?"

December 30 (Early Morning)

Agent Hong was busy with the ambassador and minister, and he needed some way to get them home, so naturally, I couldn't use the van to get to the hospital. Luckily, the restaurant was a block away from a nightclub, which made the location popular for taxis waiting to haul some poor, drunk souls home. By the time I was able to hail one down, it was around 3am. The new moon had just passed into a crescent, which painted the sky a shadowy version of itself. Dark clouds barreled across the skies as if to follow me to Jenny.

Dr. Yang greeted me at the front desk. "Frank? Nice to meet you." She seemed annoyed, probably from waiting. "We tried contacting you earlier, but we were unable to reach you."

"How's Jenny? I just want to know she's safe, and I'll be on my way."

"Your wife drove at dangerously high speeds in the middle of the city and sustained some pretty serious injuries. It's almost a miracle she didn't hit anybody. We operated on her in the evening, and she was semi-stabilized about an hour ago. She may not live past sunrise."

Instinctually, I gave her a look of disgust after hearing the words "your wife" about Jenny after so long, but I couldn't blame her. "Can I see her now?"

She glanced at my outfit with a look of concern. "Right this way. She asked specifically for you, she even gave us your number while being wheeled in and again when she awoke."

Jenny was covered in wires and cords, seemingly tangling her in a medical spiderweb. Why she referred to me as her husband was beyond me, and even more confusing was why she made me her emergency contact. The doctor had allowed me to stay with her until she awoke, which may have been because they knew I was a government official. Regardless, I was thankful to be there when she opened her eyes.

"Frank?" Jenny muttered. "I was worried you wouldn't show."

"What are you doing here?" I whispered. "You're supposed to have returned to the United States. And what's this business about me being your husband?"

"I saw you were doing some browsing the other night, so I decided to pay you a visit. Everything was going well until…" Jenny motioned me closer and began whispering in my ear. "I was followed. I had to do something drastic to get them off of me, so I got myself in the hospital. They wouldn't let me see anyone unless they were my immediate family, but this is important."

"You did this to yourself? What could be so important to risk your life over?"

"The truth," she said weakly. "The Party is self-serving, above all. When I saw you doing your 'research,' I was elated because I knew you had realized something, possibly that the Party shouldn't be in power."

"What you're talking about could be considered high treason. For all I know, you could be a double agent, ready to capture me."

"That language," Jenny slowly processed. "You're paranoid that someone knows or will know about what you've done."

"Besides the point," I redirected. "What else did you want to tell me?"

"That there is so much more than what you discovered. Detainment camps, massacres, systematic discrimination, even computer screen and camera control, all cover-ups by the Party."

"You could say other countries are doing the same," I mentioned skeptically. "What makes China any different?"

"Because what's happening in Hong Kong is just a fraction of the corruption that you're involved in." She stared me down with a firm, yet whispery voice. "You have the power to do what's right. Learn about the world and how to save it."

"Fine, let's assume this is true, tell me about it."

"Mistreatment of citizens for religious beliefs in Xinjiang? Banning Hong Kong citizens from elections for their political stances? Or even the free, open internet you accessed the other day, restricted in China? The list goes on."

"I could list a thousand violations by the US," I dismissed. The Party is for the betterment of the people, I thought to myself. "You're wasting my time."

"Just because it happened in the US, doesn't make it fine. Change begins when we outlaw our inhumane standards, as it should be, and we can do that now."

"You could get hurt from what you're telling me now," I reminded her. "Worse, what if someone from the Party hears?"

Jenny looked around her. "Do you know what it's like to be followed? To know that somebody is suspecting you of treason? They knew what I was doing, this has to be them."

"Now you're the one sounding paranoid. You think someone tried to assassinate you for coming to tell me all this?"

She began tearing up. "How do you not believe me? After I blacked out, I woke up with these. I know my crash wasn't this bad, somebody got to me before the ambulance. These aren't common injuries, or maybe even possible from what I did." Jenny used her strength to sit upright, causing apparent strain on her body and loud blaring from her heart monitor. Now out of breath, Jenny chose her words wisely. "I'm dying, I knew the risk coming here. Please, Frank, if not for me, for the kids. They're safe with some friends now, but they still shouldn't debate whether their father is a good man."

Knowing our kids were somewhere safe put me a little more at ease. However, the escalation of going from doing the Party's bidding, to compromise, to treason was nigh unthinkable. As much as I should despise them for possibly allowing this to happen, why could I not bring myself to that?

"Frank," Jenny started again as I pondered in silence. "It's not enough to stand around silently as this unfolds and say 'I didn't pull the trigger, so it doesn't matter.' You have to say 'I did what I could to stop it.'"

Jenny was paler than the moonlit room, having a harder time breathing with every word she spoke. She was also visibly losing energy, so I helped her lay down. "I think you should rest, honey."

"You haven't called me that in ages," she laughed as she slipped asleep. As she went gently into that good night, doctors rushed in to attempt to save her, to no avail. I was swiftly rushed out to make room for the essential workers; however, I could hear the pronouncement of death from the door.

Doctor Yang caught me on my way out of the hospital. "Mr. Zhong, frankly, it's customary for the next of kin to decide what to do with the deceased next. I realize this must be traumatizing, but can we expect you to return soon to discuss it?"

"Yeah," I emotionlessly responded. "She was an organ donor, I believe? Use any of it if it'll help someone somewhere. For her body, send it back to America to our oldest son, and he'll figure it out."

Yang seemed taken aback by my inexpressiveness. "Very well," she said, handing me a clipboard of documents. "Sign these and put your son's contact information at the bottom. You may turn this in at the front desk when you're done. Have a nice night, sir."

I could practically see the annoyance and frustration seeping through her face. Left alone, I realized I didn't know Yunzi's information. Hoping for the best, I wrote down a friend in America's phone number and took a taxi home. Whether or not Jenny died delirious, I didn't want to know. It'd be better if I left it there and let her rest in peace. With any luck, this was all a bad dream I could sleep off.

December 30

With today being the deadline, I knew it would be imperative to seek a confession. If I were to fail, no doubt Agent Hong would take over my position and take the glory for himself. Kai was locked behind the isolation chamber since he was uncooperative during our last encounter. With him back in the interrogation room, I needed to get information out of him, or the Party would have my head.

"Kai, I'm afraid our time together is almost up," I reminded him and myself. If we do not come to a compromise today, you will be transferred to one of my colleagues, and I cannot guarantee anything that happens after that."

"I've already told you everything I can, Frank," he insisted. "I'm not involved, neither are my friends, in a terrorist plot."

"All I need you to do is tell us that you were conspiring against the Party, which I know you were."

"That's just as good as admitting I was wrong," Kai sighed. "If I tell you that or anything of the sort, I'll just be another example of the Party breaking a human for its self-preservation."

"You and I have spent far too much time talking about your thoughts on the Party, rather than the matter at hand," I told him. "I played your game, now I'm begging you, tell me something. Throw someone under the bus, I don't care. If you don't come up with something, the Party will make somebody take the fall with you to save face."

Kai considered this. "If I say something, I get thrown in jail for God knows how long, alongside one of my friends. If I say nothing, I still disappear, but possibly alone, possibly with some random person. If I compromise, no matter what I ask for, it's either not guaranteed or temporary."

I was dumbfounded, left in a corner. After a week, I turned up with nothing. I failed the Party. A strange wave of relief overtook me, although what precisely about the current situation that calmed me was unclear. "Kai," I started. "What do you believe makes a 'good man?'"

Confused by the query, Kai sat back in his chair. "Excuse me? What do you mean by that?"

Confused by the query, Kai sat back in his chair. "Excuse me? What do you mean by that?"

"I mean, from your perspective," I clarified. "What constitutes a 'good man?' Is it his ideals? His will? His actions? His past? Surely from your point-of-view, you're one of these 'good men,' so what does that mean to you?"

He pondered, searching his brain for the right words to form. "I suppose... I would have to say that a 'good man' acts for the greater good, not because it benefits him, but because it's simply the decent way to live."

"As expected of an opinion," I added. "A matter of perspective."

"Were you satisfied with my answer, officer?"

Why did I ask him such a question? To satisfy myself? To reason with my actions? Possibly questions destined to never be answered. "Very much so. I'll return you to your chambers. This may be the last time we see each other, so farewell. I pray the next agent humanizes you as I have."

After having Kai escorted back to his chamber, I found Jian and asked him to pull up the case transfer forms and print them. "This is a high-value case," he reminded me. "Why are you just giving it up?"

"I missed the deadline," I shrugged. "Where's Agent Hong? I'll need his signature."

"I think I saw him in the viewing gallery of the interrogation room."

"Oh, no," I realized. "He probably saw me give up in that room, what a failure I am." My head hung low in shame. Sure enough, I found him there, packing his items.

"Frank!" He excitedly shook my hand. "Excellent job, comrade. Thank you for transferring the job to me, it'll be quite the case to crack."

"How do you plan on doing that?"

Agent Hong looked around us, checking out the halls for any eavesdroppers. After shutting the door behind him for complete silence, he turned to me and gravely inquired, "Have you ever heard of the 'White Maw?'"

I shook my head. "What's that?"

Hong began to escort himself off the premises. "Let's save that for tomorrow. I have preparations to make." He then saw the signature form in my hands. "Give that here."

The agent's signature was large and bold with near-perfect calligraphy. "See you tomorrow."

December 30 (Late Night)

Returning to my apartment, feeling dejected and bored, I began to browse the open Internet via the contraband laptop. I found many websites, cataloging the most important ones. I found myself favoriting many obscene sites, following a rabbit hole of sensual pictures and videos with the feeling of loneliness and self-hatred looming over me.

By nightfall, I had desensitized myself to the bottomless pit of promiscuity and found myself more interested in other matters. Like what Jenny had said, information that was once censored was made free for me to trek. The deeper I dug, the more unsure I was of who I was, what I stood for, and what I fought for. While some of the information was clearly falsified, others shed light in directions in which there was none.

New Year's Eve

"Happy New Year's Eve, Frank!" Jian smiled warmly. "Any plans for the new decade?"

I rubbed my eyes, sore from staring at the LED panels of the laptop screen. "Maybe I'll quit this miserable job," I mumbled.

"Ha!" Jian laughed, far too loud. "Always the jokester with you. By the way, Agent Hong is waiting for you in the staff area, probably to talk about case matters."

Lounging alone, I found Hong fingering through some files and flipping through his notebook. "Frank, just the man I wanted to see."

"What do you need?" I spied on a case he had in his suit pocket. "Is that the 'Maw?'"

Noticing this, he chuckled. "Oh, no, no, no. This is a tool of interrogation. I just wanted to ask you to assist me in ordering the guards around, I don't know the protocol here."

Agent Hong had Kai thrown into the interrogation room, rougher than I ever ordered. Once I settled myself in the viewing gallery, I had front row seats to the show. Kai was visibly nervous, unsure of who he was facing or how to react.

Hong sat across from Kai from the table. "I know who you are, Wu. I read your-"

"Clearly not close enough," Kai remarked. "It's Ng."

Enraged, Hong punched Kai so hard, the chair flew to the side and nearly toppled the poor teen. "You dare talk back to me, you punk? It's this kind of talk that'll get you killed. I understand you're not much of a confessor, so I'll make this quick. My job is to break you by whatever means necessary. You had it easy with Zhong, and that's over. Why? Because I am here."

Kai spat his blood-mixed saliva into Hong's face. It was almost comedic if it weren't for the smug look on the agent's face once again dissolving into pure hatred. The burly man uppercut Kai in his chair, flinging him like a ragdoll. I could only pray Kai would lose consciousness.

The stubborn boy was steadfast, clearly not losing hope.

"I'm unbreakable," he proclaimed.

"Is that so?" Hong brought out his cartridge and placed it on the table, making it visible from the gallery. Inside was a syringe and three bottles of unknown origin. "Pick a number, one to three."

"Screw you," Kai groaned. Still on the ground, he coughed up some blood.

"Yellow it is," the agent sighed. Picking the mustard vial from the trio, Hong only needed a few drops for deadly potency. Kai thrashed in his seat, creating difficulty for Agent Hong, who was trying to find an optimal injection point.

Selecting the arm to start, the agent single-handedly stabilized the teenager for a brief moment. The syringe liquid caused Kai's skin to rash and bubble, clearly causing excruciating pain in his bicep. Although agonizing, it wasn't nearly enough for him to pass out, much to the agent's delight.

New Year's Eve, 2013 (Six Years Ago)

"Hurry, Daddy, hurry!" cried little Guan.

"Yunzi, can you unlock the door for your brother? I need to unload the luggage," I asked.

"Sure, sure, come on, kid," Yunzi reluctantly responded.

"Be nicer to him," Jenny commanded. "Family takes care of family."

"Don't forget, Dad," Yunzi called out behind him. I raised my head from the trunk of the car. "I want to talk to you about something before we tune into the countdown."

"Right, right," I pretended to remember. "I'll be there in a second, but put Guan to sleep first." As the two brothers disappeared into the doorframe, I handed one of the bags to Jenny. "Those kids, now they're so eager to come home."

"Guan always gets homesick after vacations," Jenny shrugged. "More importantly, I hope you think about what I said."

"What else am I going to find other than what I've already been briefed on?"

"You're missing the 'human element.' Until you take the time to understand what the people actually going through the event are thinking, you won't accomplish much, not only as an interrogation officer but also as a person."

It was clear Jenny was adamant about getting me to research the inner workings of the Party. I doubted her since I was so focused on proving my skills and loyalty to the country. "When I have the time, honey. I'm guessing it's reasons like that which got you guys hung up on those libraries."

"Knowledge is power, Frank. It doesn't help that the internet is largely filtered here at home, while there's free access in America."

"Filters and regulation keep order, the internet should be no different. The Party knows what's best." I unloaded the last bag and walked it over to the house. I found Yunzi waiting for me in the living room, the television tuned to the Beijing New Year's celebration.

"I'll go check in on Guan," said Jenny, reading the room. "Listen to your son, Frank," she whispered as she disappeared up the stairs.

I sat next to Yunzi, who was a tall, skinny, college-bound teenager at the time. Sitting next to him, I noticed how small he was in comparison to me, furthered by the fact he looked as if he were trying to shrink into the sofa. "So, son, what is it?"

"I want us to move," he blurted out. "To America. I don't care what state or city, but America, even if it's only me going there for college. I just don't want to be here."

"You're ridiculous," I replied. "There's nothing for you there that you can't find here."

"That's not the problem," he sobbed. "I don't feel safe here, why does it always feel like this? Like the government controls everything? Like there's no me, only the state-allowed me." He pointed at the television, with the celebratory broadcast. "Even that, it feels so fake, like a show just so the people in charge look better."

"You're my son, you live here, you cannot ask me to uproot this family and start new in another country," I raised my voice. "You sound so much like your mother, she's brainwashing you."

"Mom did nothing like that!" Yunzi defended. "She listens, she understands, she's a better parent than-"

I backhanded him across the face. "What's wrong with you? No respect, no discipline, only rebellion. First, you order me, as my son, to leave the land of our ancestors. Then, you insult me in my own home. You disgrace our family name."

Clearly upset, Yunzi rushed upstairs to his room. Swiftly, Jenny ran downstairs and slapped me across the cheek. "What the hell was that? You're a sad excuse for a father."

"What did you say, you hag?" I lashed out. "He needs to be disciplined, or he'll turn into a street rat. The ungrateful child thinks he can just leave us."

"Frank," Jenny sighed.

"Yeah?"

"I want a divorce."

New Year's Eve, 2019 (Late Night)

It had been just hours after Frank left the viewing gallery before Agent Hong and his team of guards dragged the unconscious Kai out of the interrogation room. A faint morning mist began to cover the grounds of the compound, and dew lined the frame of the windows. By the time Kai had come back to his senses, he found himself in the center of a plain white room with a steel window, stuck within a small glass prison just a few tiles wide. With his face leaning against one side of the window, his feet scrunched against the other.

Behind those full windows sat Frank and his superiors, with Ambassador Volkov and Minister Nam among them. Of them, Frank was the only one there trembling, afraid for Kai's life. Like a sick theatre, "the White Maw" was designed with velvet seats lined behind the stainless window to giddily await the next fate of the next soul who enters.

Frank shifted in his seat uncomfortably, to which the minister noticed. "First time?"

"That obvious? How secretive is this?"

"This is the White Maw, so of course, you need some of the top clearance in the homeland."

"Is this room designed for what I think it is?"

The man grinned from ear to ear. "I'm not one for spoiling surprises."

Frank turned as pale as the Maw's walls. Still trembling, Frank began to rock back and forth as he attempted to steady himself. The still of the Maw that Kai sat in was broken by Agent Hong, with a clipboard in hand and cigar in mouth. Hong walked up to the trapped Kai in discontent.

"Kai Ng. You stand guilty for high treason against the Communist Party, China itself, and its glorious citizens. You have the information we seek, that of the names and hideouts of your co-conspirators. Speak, or you will face further consequence."

Kai was steadfast, even as his knees were bent in an unnatural form. "You can't break me." Frank took a second to analyze the wounds that covered Kai's body. While some were a result of Frank's interrogations, most were now from Hong and his injections. Blisters, skin flaps, and swollen patches covered every part of his arms and legs, spreading to most of his torso.

Agent Hong put his cigar out on his clipboard. "Can't I?" He then motioned to the one-sided mirror where a guard rushed out to an undisclosed location.

Frank bit his lip, still as confused and afraid as to what is happening as Kai was. Ambassador Nam moved to fill the seat next to Frank. "Officer Zhong. I believe some time ago, you were warned that the Party will never tolerate failure. I should also remind you we do not tolerate the accessing of illegal information on private web browsers. Today marks such. You will be reprimanded after this reminding viewing experience is over."

"Reminding? Of what? And how did you know that?"

"To never cross the people. To never commit a crime in the name of yourself." Volkov stared at him for a second before laughing. "Oh, heavens, I understand. You thought your punishment would be this? No, this is strictly reserved for the foulest rejecters of the law. As for your little insurrection, Agent Hong searched your apartment the night before our meeting and found the laptop. A simple confiscation will do for now."

Frank no longer feared for his punishment, as he anxiously dreaded whatever was to come for Kai. Finally, the guard returned with a man in chains and a black bag on his head. Agent Hong removed the bag to reveal a bloodied senior citizen.

"Father!" Kai cried.

Frank despaired, quietly choking on tears. Agent Hong then unlatched his sidearm, with it still holstered. "Now, although you may not fear death, I ask you, does your father? What say you, Mr. Fang Ng?"

Fang, who was barely able to speak, mumbled broken and indiscernible phrases, most likely due to the broken hinge on his jaw and swollen tongue. Every attempted sentence simply amounted to saliva and blood spattering on the floor.

"Touching words," mocked the Agent.

"He has nothing to do with this," sobbed Kai. "Leave him be."

"If you do not tell us what we want to hear, your father will perish. We have a dozen other known associates of yours lined up outside faced against the compound wall. Every time you deny us, we deny their further existence. If, after all of you choose to spill all of this blood in the name of your revolution, then you will have my respect. Then, will you have my permission to die."

Kai pounded on the windows, attempting to break them to reach his father to no avail. Fang began to keel over, falling to the floor due to fatigue. Kai could do nothing but despair, carefully watching his father's mouth word one phrase, "I'm proud of you."

Agent Hong walked over to step on Fang's face to make sure no scheming would appear. He turned to Kai with a smirk. "Take a good look around the Maw, child. You either leave with your life or your dignity, but never both." The agent then unholstered his weapon and began. The agent began, "Five."

"You can't do this," Kai pleaded.

"Four."

"I signed up for this, not him." Kai's begs became increasingly drowned out by a ringing in his ears. Frank continued to watch in horror.

"Three." Hong picked Fang up by the collar, pressing his face against the glass on Kai's capsule.

"Father… I have failed you." Kai matched his hand up to his father's, which was now barely scratching the window.

"Two."

"Wait," he cried. "I'll tell you anything." Agent Hong threw Fang across the room, fracturing his elbow upon impact. The guard then escorted him out. "Please, just guarantee my father's safety. Be at least that decent."

"Your fates will be matched, I assure you. Tell us what you know."

A curtain began to fall, separating the spectators from the stage window. Jian had brought champagne for the room and glasses per Nam's request, which were being distributed in a celebratory manner. The cheers that filled that room were nearly loud enough to penetrate the walls to Kai. Meanwhile, Frank was far less joyful than his peers.

As he stared into his glass, Frank pondered to himself. Fiddling with the cup, Nam approached him. "What's with the sadness? We saved the president! Be merry!"

Frank stopped him. "How have we allowed ourselves to commit this in the name of justice?"

"Ourselves? No, no, Frank. This was all thanks to you and the Agent. There's nothing to worry about. Truth at any cost, that's what you signed up for. As a plus, when the State says it's legal, it is. You wanted that promotion, you'll get it." Frank began to tear up. Misunderstanding the emotions, the officer clinked glasses with him as a toast.

Not noticing he was once again alone, Frank began to mumble to himself. "He took mere minutes to do what I could not in days. Could it be that I refused to cross a line I should have?"

Agent Hong burst into the room with bravado and applause. As the room chanted his name as if he were a war hero, he asked that Frank join him. "Truly," he started. "This is our collective victory."

"You saw it through," Frank congratulated. "I assure you that this win is yours, Agent."

The agent looked at him with confusion. "Did you forget? Take a look at this." Hong handed Frank his notebook, small and brown, with a little leather tassel locking the secrets inside. The cover was embroidered with a hammer and sickle. "Open it, comrade."

Frank fumbled the book open. The pages were yellowed from time; however, it was clear which notes were the most recently added. An entire section was dedicated to the "Operation Peacetime," a codename no doubt bestowed upon by the Party for this particular case. Every page was cataloged with Kai's thoughts and ideas, leading to his known friends and family. In his own time, the agent had found nearly every close associate.

Hong placed his arm around Frank's shoulder. "It was your help, your information that had helped me apprehend the people I needed. I herded them like sheep thanks to you, now outside those doors are a dozen of his potential co-conspirators. If he had continued to deny their involvement, I simply would have brought them in one by one and done what I had to. What an embarrassment that would have been."

Frank, although skeptical at the Agent's words, pretended to smile for the room. "What will you do with them now?"

"You know as well as I do what that mound by the east gate is for. What, did you think any of those criminals would be getting away? They're taken care of, I assure you."

"And the father?"

"Did you expect he would be walking out of here? Never would the Party take such risks of public outcry. We must remain vigilant against such contingencies, which is why frequently, some people seem to…" The agent trailed off as he remembered various faces and encounters from the past. "Nevertheless, the father has now joined them."

New Year's Day (Early Morning)

Kai carried himself outside the compound structure. Frank held his gun threateningly against Kai's back, ensuring that the teenager would not move a single foot out of line. Frank's eyesight aligned with the side of the structure, where a foul stench originated from.

"Move," Frank barked in his voice that went unused in what seemed to be a lifetime.

"I can't." Kai stood back, arched against the gun uncomfortably. His legs shifted like crumbling columns, mixing his emotions of crippling fear and spiteful anxiousness with physical pain.

"You should know well that the answer is simply unacceptable." Frank tightened his grip hard enough to make the faintest creak of the bolts on it. "I'm begging you, please do not make me use this."

"You're a good man, Frank." Kai began to tiptoe towards the ghastly stench. "Thank you."

"For what?"

"For actually treating me like a human being, even if it was for a few hours. I wish we had met sooner."

Holding back, Frank began to lower his gun, despite still pushing Kai forward. Beyond the corner was a dirt mound, seeded with rotting meat. Many smaller hills led away from the larger one, skewed across for about twenty feet in miniature rows a few inches tall. Each row was just a few feet wide, just enough to squeeze a human into them. Past the rows was the gated perimeter surrounding the entire facility. However, on this side was the eastern exit, one of the least utilized wings of the site. Entirely abandoned and isolated from other facility areas except for one observatory on the second floor, the eastern exit led to a desolate road.

Frank pointed to the horizon the road led to. "You wanted to return home, so I will give it to you. This road leads straight into the heart of Hong Kong, so take it as a present from me."

Kai turned to unamused, pointing towards the disappe-

-aring officer's footprints and bloodstains. "Et tu, Brute?"

"There was no way out for you, and you knew that. It was either leave in a body bag or on this road. Most prisoners never got the choice."

"What will happen to those other guys? The men locked with me."

"Do you really care? Run. You're free as a bird. The Party always upholds its promises."

"How do you do that, speak all that crap into existence? Must get tiring."

"Mock me if you will, however, you are in no position to do much else. At least this way, you can pretend that I might miss and that you'll actually get that sunrise escape you dream of."

Kai turned towards the city in the distance, imagining the hero's welcome on every road. "It's a nice dream, isn't it?"

Frank grunted, in agreement, choking on his emotions. "Go."

"You're a good man, Frank. What I would give to be born as your son in the next life."

Frank's tears swelled from the beginning of the sentence. Streaks began to run across them by the end. Frank could see Kai sprinting afar through his gentle sobbing, not yet out of range of his punishment still in hand. As Frank aimed down his sights, he knew the trigger had to be pulled. The adventure was over now, and it was his job to make sure there were no witnesses. His arms sagged with the weight on his chest, now extending to his extremities.

Kai began disappearing into the light, morning fog. "How disappointing." Agent Hong approached Frank from behind, who was pointing a long-range rifle in the distance. "Move."

Frank turned to the agent. "He's just a kid, barely even old enough to drink. Let him go."

Hong was disgusted by this response. "Right," he remarked as he aimed down his sights.

Burning with hate, Frank punched Hong in the face, forcing the agent to drop the rifle and allowing Kai to disappear entirely. Frank then pulled his gun on the agent. "I said, 'let him go.'"

"Now what?" Hong laughed. "No one left to save you."

With nothing left to lose, Frank pulled the trigger. Now there was something, someone worth dying for.

Author's Note

Dear Reader,

This story first began its conception in September 2019. It broke my heart to see that so many people of the United States were unaware of the situation in Hong Kong. As I continued to observe the events unfold, I was determined to write and develop a narrative from the perspectives of the average protester and the police. I am not a citizen of Hong Kong, or of any country in Asia for that matter. However, as one who lives in a democratic nation, I believed that merely standing by without acting would be hypocritical of me. While I could not travel to Hong Kong myself to ask for justice, I could do what I can by advocating for people to educate themselves on the issue. Suprisingly enough, during the winter, I was eventually inspired by videos of Christmas protests and protesters singing songs about freedom, namely the United States national anthem and "Do You Hear the People Sing?" from *Les Miserables*.

Since 2019, the world has changed. Situations across the world rise and fall like the tide and contemporary events regularly overtake each other. Despite that, peace and freedom will always be a dream of someone in the world, whether it be the cry of a single person or an entire nation. Stories are forever timeless, as well as what they reflect. Changing times will never take away from the struggle the people of Hong Kong have suffered and endured. Even as represented in a fictional character in a fictional version of our world, their story can persevere and teach the world what it means to be free.

Sincerely,

Huang Yanhong

作者注

亲爱的读者

这个故事是我在2019年9月开始萌生动念想创作的一本书，当我看到那么多美国人对香港的惨状不知情的时候～我心碎了。

我继续观察香港的事件被报道出来，我就下定决心要写并制作一本描述一位普通的「香港抗议者」与「香港警察」的观点。我自身不是一位香港居民，也不是其他亚洲国家的居民。但是；作为一位住在民主政治国家的人，我相信我不应该只做一位旁观者。虽然，我无法自己启程到香港去做抗议者，一起陪同香港居民为正义而战；但我能尽我所能的去传播这个事件给更多人去关注和学习香港的真实状况。

冬天的時候，我听完美国的国歌叫《星条旗之歌》和一首叫《民眾的呐喊》兩首歌曲后；我就有了写这本书的启发。

自2019年起，这个世界变化了许多，全球的政治问题与社会问题都在大起大落中；再加上许多不一般发生在这个时代的问题，他们都在互相争抢着被重视的机会。尽管世界有怎么样的走向，和平和自由会一直是一个人或一整个国家的梦想。故事与故事间的含义是永恒的，时代的变化并不会带走香港人在为自己挺身而出抗议时的苦日子。即使是用虚构人物去代表相似于我们世界中的虚构世界；他们的故事也能永久的教育世人「自由真正的含义」。

真切的黃言泓，译：蔡宛玲

Acknowledgements

I'd like to thank a couple special people, not only for their help in the making of this book, but for encouraging me to be a better person.

Gavin, thank you for being the first reader, your feedback was especially helpful and inspiring for me.

Jaden, thank you for help on the cover design, I wouldn't have been able to realize this book to it's fullest without you.

The M.D. and Collective, thank you for being my closest friends thoughout the years.

Tyler, Jon, Kate, and Heidi, thank you for being my teachers over the years, you inspire me to better myself and my writing.

Amilie, thank you for your endless support and help whenever I need it, you're the most amazing person ever.

Mom and Dad, thank you for everything you've ever done for me, I'll never be able to fully express my appreciation.

You, the reader, for allowing me the chance to prove my writing abilities. This is my first book and I hope you enjoyed it.

www.ingramcontent.com/pod-product-compliance
Lightning Source LLC
LaVergne TN
LVHW011853060526
838200LV00054B/4314